ZSOLT KEREKES

Alexander Woyte and the Goblins

the goblins have kidnapped the 4 year old Alexander,
the hunt is on to get him back

First published by Zsolt Kerekes 2023

First edition

This book was professionally typeset on Reedsy.
Find out more at reedsy.com

thanks to Andrew and his family – for inspiring this story

Contents

Foreword

It's modern times (as modern as they ever get) in the pointy churched sleepy village of Privett in Hampshire, Olde England.

No one believes in goblins any more. But once every 70 years the goblin king who lives under the Old Bookshop in Petersfield sends out scouts to find a replacement human puppy to kidnap. Ideally a fair haired boy aged 4. Alexander looks like a perfect candidate. His life hasn't been the same since.

Since its publication in 2001 this story has been read by tens of thousands of readers. Now available for the first time as a phone friendly ebook

1

Alexander Woyte and the Goblins

Privett is a sleepy village in Hampshire in Old England. It's a very traditional place and nothing exciting ever happens there. Or at least that's what most people think...

The people who live there keep quiet about what really goes on, because they don't want lots of reporters disturbing their peace.

If the TV news people knew what an exciting place it really was, they would probably keep a camera crew there all the time. Yet still they might see nothing. Because the most exciting things happen at night, when all the good people of Privett are tucked up in bed.

This is a story about Alexander Woyte, a young boy living in Jibb Cottage, in Privett. He didn't expect to have an adventure. And this is how it began...

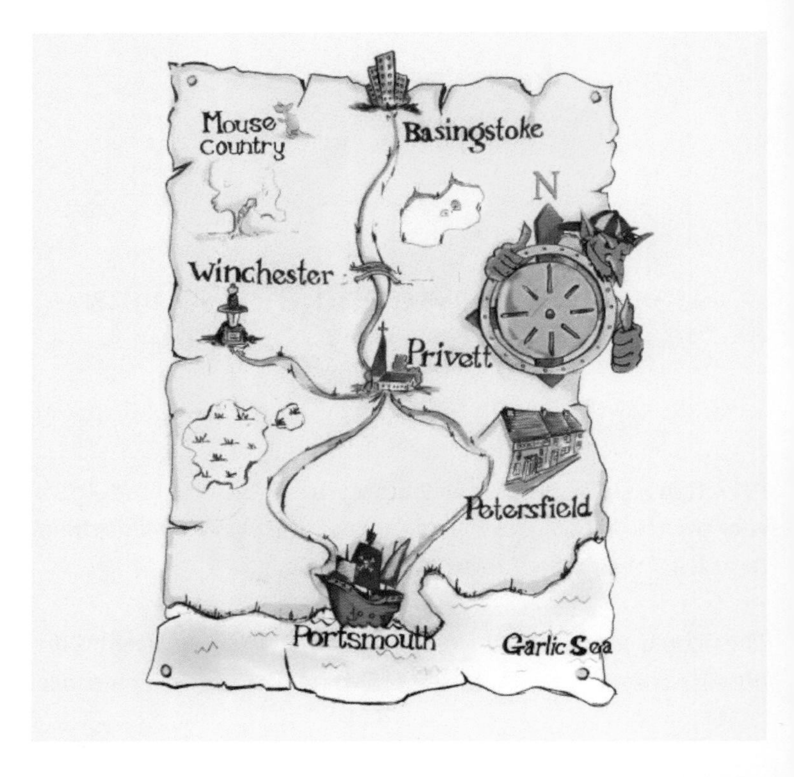

Gunnar, king of the Old Wessex Division of the goblins, had a problem. His old slave, Eric, had died. That usually happened to humans once they became about seventy or eighty, and there was nothing you could do about it, except get a new one. The king had grown quite fond of Eric who had been captured by the goblins in 1925 as a young boy. It was best to catch them young. There had been a hue and cry. There always is, when a man child disappears. You can't hush these things up. Some people blamed the gypsies. Others said: perhaps he had wandered off to join the circus.

But no one ever thought of blaming the goblins... That's because 1925 was the twentieth century and people didn't believe in such things any more. Gunnar's great grandfather, Aleric the goblin had once met King Arthur, and now most people thought Arthur was just a legend.

Eric's parents had been very upset, but then after a few years they had another son. They never really gave up hope of finding Eric again, and just to be on the safe side, because they were country folk and remembered some of the old traditions, they used to leave presents like milk and chocolate outside the back door at night to keep on the good side of the fairies.

"You're mad" their neighbors used to say. "It's only being eaten by rats, or hedgehogs."

Something did used to come and take the chocolate every night. But even though Eric's parents took turns in watching to see what it was, they always fell asleep at the critical time. In fact it was Gunnar's minions who collected the offerings, and goblins are good at casting sleep waves when they don't want to be disturbed. But Gunnar always remembered to give Eric his fair share of the goodies. It wasn't such a bad life being the king's slave. Eric was happy, and soon forgot all about his first home.

In 1939 there was another war. Chocolate and milk were rationed. So Eric's parents stopped leaving these gifts outside. But sometimes food would go missing inside the house. And even vanish from inside a closed tin. They knew it wasn't mice. You can hear mice, or see where they've been. "Eric's had another biscuit," they would say. Sometimes Eric really did have the biscuit, courtesy of Gunnar's marauding goblins. But more often it was Eric's brother who realized he could get away with midnight pantry raids without getting the blame.

Now that Eric was dead, Gunnar needed to get a replacement.

Having a human slave was one of the status symbols that went along with being the goblin king. It was traditional. This was similar to the fashion, in rich humans, of having a posy car like a BMW, or a trophy wife.

The headquarters of the Old Wessex Division of the goblins was in the tunnels beneath the old bookshop in Petersfield. If you went into the dark forgotten corners of the shop, and moved aside the dusty bookcase with the really old falling-apart books with no covers, which were hardly ever sold, you might, if you looked carefully, see the outline of a secret door which led into tunnels underground. The goblins liked living there because, if they got bored at night, they could sneak upstairs and "borrow" some of the old books. They didn't like modern writers. They even regarded Jane Austen as modern.

Gunnar's father had known Jane Austen. She was a local girl who lived in nearby Chawton. When she was writing a book called "Emma", he used to read over her shoulder. One day he complained about the picnic scene at Box Hill.

"Where are the goblins?" he asked.

In those days you always saw goblins hanging around picnics, waiting to pounce and run off with the leftovers. If they were greedy little goblins they might not actually wait for you to finish, or even start your carefully planned picnic. And if you were very unlucky you might end up eating little more than a few crumbs yourself. That's why Gunnar's Goblin Hammers became such a popular method of picnic pest control. But they were invented a lot later and don't come into this story...

"Where are the goblins?" he asked again, thinking he had made a very good point by spotting a weakness in her picnic scene. It just wasn't realistic.

"Goblins? Schmoglins! This story is about people! Nice polite people, who aren't green and slimy. So... Sorry! NO goblins! It would be an altogether quite different book, if there were goblins at the picnic on Box Hill. It would be.." She hesitated and chose her words with the exquisite care and precision that only a great novelist in her prime can achieve. "It would be yucky!"

Gentle reader, Jane sometimes spoke somewhat differently to the way she wrote. Quite like an ordinary person in fact.

"Oh dear" thought Jane, who always reacted badly when anyone criticized her writing. "I've upset him now."

She didn't mean to do that. Jane liked Gunnar's dad a lot and thought he was a real cutie, for an ugly goblin. So to make up, she wrote him a special secret book which she called "Goblin Park." She also wrote a different version for humans. But "Goblin Park" became one of the old goblin's most favorite stories. He would read it out loud to anyone who cared to listen. Or to anyone who had heard it a hundred times before but didn't run away fast enough.

"Jane Austen wrote this book for me!" He'd declare proudly. "Look at the dedication. - Goblin Park, inspired by, and dedicated to my favorite old goblin king. Lots of kisses (not real ones - just pretend). Love Jane."

He thought it was her best book. She really knew how to write about goblins in a wicked mischievous way. Shame it was never published in the human world. Also shame that she wasn't a boy. She would have made quite a good goblin slave, but that would have interfered with her career as a writer.

In the old days, when the goblins wanted to solve a difficult problem, they all used to assemble in a goblin meeting just outside the bookshop. Nowadays, the best place to go was over the road from the bookshop in the car park outside Waitrose. They usually held their meetings at about three o'clock in the morning. That way it was likely there would be less people strolling about to notice. The few people who did happen to stumble across a large group of goblins on a wild winter's night usually assumed they had been drinking too much at the pub before. The Salvation Army always got some new recruits after a goblin meet.

"It was seeing them wee green ugly devils in the Petersfield car park as made me sign the pledge" said an old Sally Army Captain (now retired). He hadn't touched anything stronger than a home made lemonade since. And he had moved to Basingstoke, just to be on the safe side.

Although, like many supermarkets, the Waitrose building in Petersfield was built in a horrible modern style, it did have one definite advantage. The smaller minion goblins could climb in through the air conditioning vents, and then pass out packets of ready made sandwiches, beer and crisps.

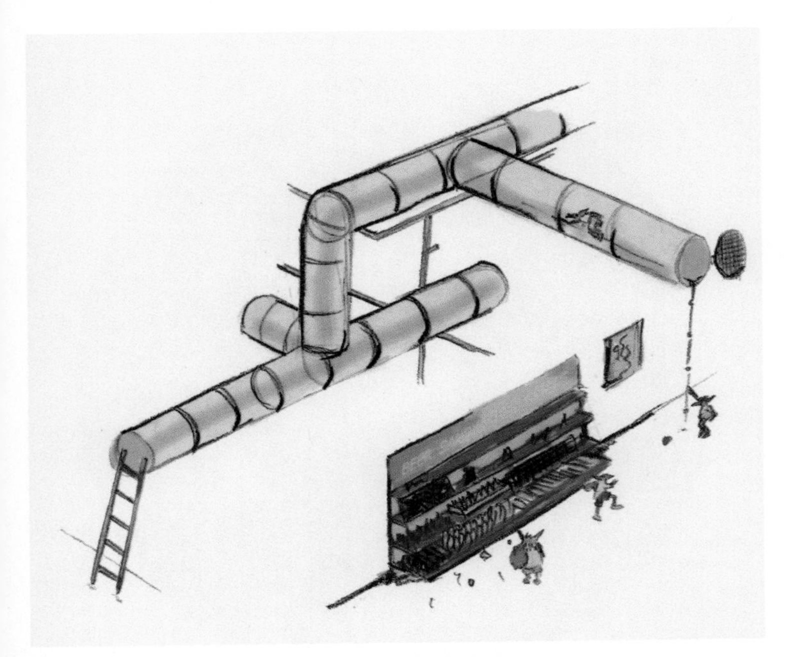

On those occasions when the security cameras in Waitrose did get good clear pictures of the goblin minions walking across the food shelves, the chief of security muttered - "If I ever get my hands on the practical jokers who tamper with these tapes, they're for it."

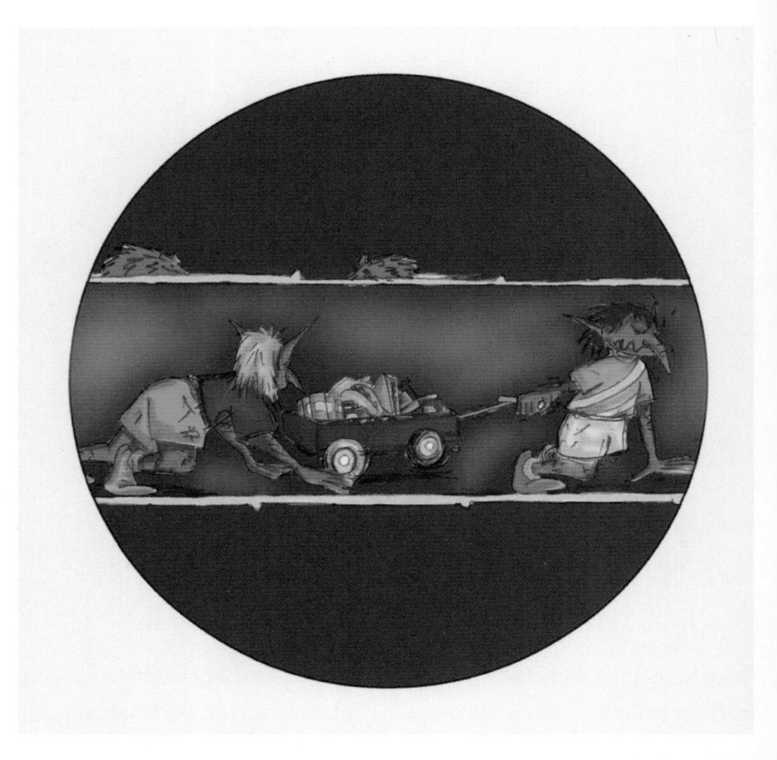

When all the goblins and the local mischievous animals were gathered together, the goblin king explained the situation.

"Some of you are too young to remember what Eric looked like when he first came here, but my ideal candidate for a new slave would be someone similar to what he was when he started. A young boy, ideally no more than about four years old, with blonde hair. Preferably living in the countryside hereabouts. Not too close, or the police might discover our hideout. But not too far away either, because we've got to carry him back here in one night. Now does anyone know of any suitable candidates?"

There was a cockerel in the car park. He didn't have much of a brain, but he liked hanging out with the goblins at night because they had good parties. Neighbors in the area always assume when they hear a cock crowing in the middle of the night that it's got something to do with the full moon, or the light from a passing car. As if a cock can't tell the difference between those things and the rising of the dawn. Rubbish! When goblins have a party they always get to the stage in their proceedings when they start to sing. The older ones sing folk songs like "Greensleeves". Some of the younger ones like rock and roll. There's nothing like a bunch of drunken goblins at a karaoke night singing "Blue suede shoes" to get you in the mood.

Unfortunately cocks have a limited range when it comes to singing, and whatever they sing always seems to come out more like "Cock a doodle do." Anyway, this cock hopped up and down until he got noticed. (He was under strict instructions not to crow while in the car park, because townsfolk who aren't used to hearing this sound might get suspicious and investigate.)

"And what have you got to say for yourself Mr Cock?" asked the chairman of the goblin meeting.

"Please, sir, I think I know just the sort of person you're looking for. I used to live in the garden of a cottage where they had a little fair haired boy. He should be just the right age by now."

"What do you mean? Used to live..."

"When they discovered" the cock blushed "My hidden talents, they sent me away to the farm."

"You mean when they discovered your singing talents, more like" commented one of the younger goblins.

"OK, let's not start that" said the chairman. "Where does this boy you're talking about live?"

"Privett" said the cock, giving the young goblin an evil look as if you say "Your singing's not much better."

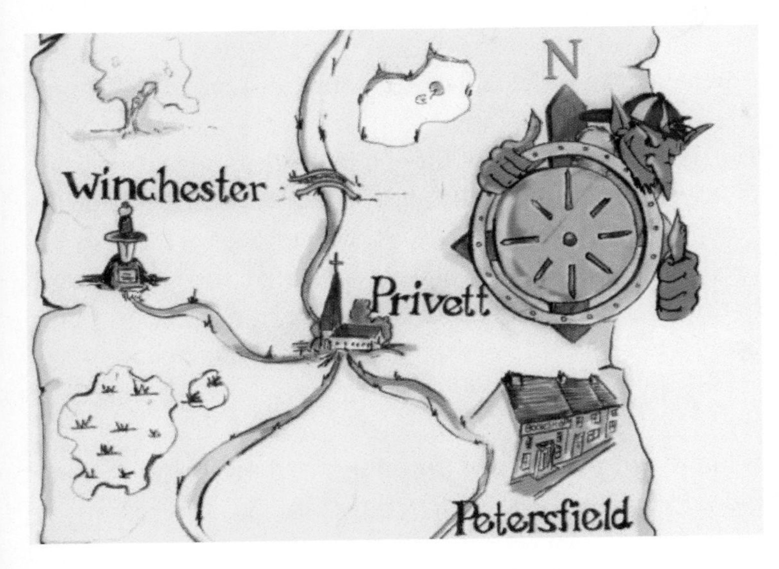

"I know where that is," said Gunnar the goblin king. "I remember them building that pointy church when I was a young lad. "That's certainly in the right area. What's the name of this young boy?"

"Alexander" said the cock. "Alexander Woyte."

"OK" said the king. "I'll send one of my minions over there tomorrow to have a look. You can give him the address."

There were no more suggestions at the meeting, so all the goblins went back into the bookshop and the animals all went home. On his way back to the tunnels, as he was passing the shelves of rare old history books, Gunnar stopped to borrow a first edition copy of Robert Louis Stephenson's book called "Kidnapped".

"Might get a few useful ideas from this" he thought.

The next morning, one of the goblin king's minions went over to Privett to spy out the lie of the land. He waited outside the group of cottages which the cock had described to him. Several cars departed with their adult occupants, on their way to work or the shops. Then, finally in the middle cottage the back door opened to reveal... a tall woman holding a baby, followed by a small Jack Russell dog, and, last of all, a smiling fair haired boy.

"That will do nicely" said the minion to himself. "Very nicely indeed."

That night Alexander's parents read him bedtime stories as usual. The last one was "Good Night Gorilla" by Peggy Rathmann.

Everyone was feeling very sleepy, and Alex was asleep before they even put him into the top of his bunk bed. Then his parents, Andrew and Joanna went downstairs, and all was quiet, as they fell asleep under the charm of a goblin spell. Even the dogs next door were quiet, and even their own little dog was quiet, and nowhere to be seen.

Just then the window in Alexander's room crept open, and in popped five goblin minions. Alex woke up. He wasn't scared. He sometimes had adventures in his dreams, and he thought this was one of them.

"Who are you?" he said.

"More to the point," said the biggest minion, who was also the chief steward "Who are you?"

"Alexander Woyte" replied Alex in his best Hampshire accent. The goblin ticked off his delivery note. "Right lads, this is the one."

Before Alex could say anything, they popped a bandage over his mouth, and four minions quickly tied him up. Then, very carefully, taking care not to bump him on the way, they lifted him out of the window, where another bunch of minions were waiting to catch him.

"Be careful" said the chief steward minion from inside. "He's very precious, and not be bumped or injured in any way in transit."

goblinrail

In a few seconds all the goblins had hopped it out of the window, which closed quietly.

Then from under the bed, a little dog appeared. It was Snoozy. She had been sleeping under the bed, which she wasn't supposed to do. But because she was already asleep, the goblin spell didn't affect her. She knew what she had to do, and raced downstairs to the sitting room where everyone was sleeping.

First she jumped onto Andrew's lap. (Andrew was Alexander's father). She licked and licked at his face. That usually worked to wake him up. But tonight it had no effect.

Then she jumped onto Joanna's lap. (Joanna was Alexander's mother). Snoozy licked and licked at her face. That usually worked to wake Joanna up. But tonight it had no effect.

Then Snoozy went over carefully to Charlie's cot. (Charlie, was Alexander's baby brother.) Snoozy licked and licked, and Charlie woke up. Charlie looked around and realized it was a long time since he had last eaten (it wasn't actually, but babies aren't very good at telling the time). Charlie saw that everyone was asleep, so he started to yell. He yelled and cried as loud as he could.

The cry of baby has a special power which is even stronger than a goblin spell. Andrew and Joanna woke up straight away. Snoozy was running around in circles very excitedly, and she wouldn't stop until someone realized what she was trying to say.

"I think that dog is trying to tell us something" said Joanna. "She's trying very hard."

Finally Snoozy managed to say "The goblins have taken Alex out the window. We've got to get him back."

"I've never heard that dog talk before" said Andrew. "Have you been giving him lessons?"

"No, wait a minute" said Joanna. "It sounds like she's talking nonsense, but I'm not so sure."

Of course a few minutes later when Snoozy had explained what she heard, and they went upstairs, they realized that Alex had gone. They also found a goblin hat, which had fallen on the floor, and Alexander's little plastic fireman toy.

"He wouldn't have gone anywhere without this" said Andrew. "He must be in trouble."

"You'll need a horse to go after them" said Joanna. "I'll phone Mervyn, and some people from the hunt. You go off to the farm."

Mervyn was Alexander's godfather and ran the local kennels and livery stable. He liked most animals and his favorite were the barn owls. But he didn't like mice or rats. If any of these rodents got caught in the grain traps, then instead of throwing the bodies away with the rubbish, as you or I might do, he would wait till dark and then put them out in the tall barn for the owl chicks. He had a way of understanding owls, and they often had little chats together, which sounded like a hoot.

Back at Jibb Cottage Andrew had never put on his coat and his boots so fast before. Just as he was going out the door, an idea struck him, and he went back inside to pick up his old cavalry sabre. It was an antique, but something told him it might come in useful, on this of all nights.

When he got to the farm, his horse Georgie was already saddled, and there were some friends from the hunt, with their hounds.

Mervyn said. "As soon as Joanna phoned, I sent my owls to do some scouting around. They can see quite well in the dark, and luckily tonight there's a full moon. Night Owl, said she could see Alexander and the goblins heading for the woods near Langrish. If they reach the woods, she'll lose their trail, but you should be able to pick it up again with the hounds. Good hunting and good luck."

Mervyn wasn't entirely convinced about the merits of fox hunting, though many of his friends were members of the famous (or infamous) Hursley Hambledon Hunt (called the HHH to distinguish them from the posier Hampshire Hunt or HH). But unlike the hunts in other parts of the home counties, the Privett branch of the HHH were mostly harmless. They spent as much time falling off their horses as chasing things. You could often spot a Privett huntsperson in mufti by their bandages.

The local foxes felt quite safe when the Privett hunt was out, because it slowed down the traffic, and most foxes in England are, in fact, killed by cars.

The only time in living memory when the Privett mob had proudly brought back a gruesome trophy, the poor old fox was already decomposing and had marks on its fur which looked suspiciously like tyre-tread. But despite their lack of success at controlling the local fox population, the Privett HHH enjoyed dressing up and charging round the countryside on their horses. And they had good parties. So their friends, who were mostly "antis", didn't mind. And this was going to be one night when nobody else could do the job.

Although Mervyn looked after horses, he wasn't a confident rider. So he stayed behind at the farm as Andrew and his party set off on their cross country pursuit guided by the swirling black shape of Night Owl.

"Toowit-toowoo. How slow are you!" she cried. And then dropping her voice shouted "Hurry up and follow me you slow coaches. The goblins have got Alex and they're getting away!"

As luck would have it, they chanced across a big fox just as they were going down the track from the farm. The fox was very surprised. It had never heard of the hunt going out at night. They must be practicing new tactics to cope against the new anti-hunting legislation that the Labour government was planning.

He'd heard about it on Fox FM. He knew that his time had come, but he was prepared to give them a good run for their money.

"Bugger off" said the lead fox hound to the fox. ""We're not chasing foxes tonight. We're hunting a little boy called Alex."

The fox didn't really believe his ears, and was still wondering if he had heard right, long after the riders and hounds disappeared out of view.

"Hunting little boys? Whatever will they think of next?" the fox wondered. "I don't think anyone is going to believe this."

Anyway, to cut a long story short, because I can see that everyone's starting to yawn...

Andrew and the hunt got to the woods following Night Owl. Then Andrew fell off his horse, and the hounds picked up the scent.

"Toowit-toowoo. Good luck to you!" Night Owl hooted, and then swooped off to hunt some baby rabbits.

Horses travel faster than goblins, so it wasn't long before they caught sight of the goblins who had kidnapped Alexander. Unfortunately for the would-be rescuers, these goblins were being met by a much larger band headed by the goblin king himself, who had come out from his dark tunnels, impatient to see how things were going.

The goblins knew they didn't have to worry too much about a couple of riders out at night, and they knew if there was a fight, they would surely win. Andrew went on ahead to speak to the goblin king, and after some discussion Gunnar suggested that, instead of everyone fighting in a pitched battle the two of them could decide things in a trial by combat. He stated his terms...

"That doesn't sound, to me, like a fair deal at all" said Andrew. "If you win, you get to keep my son, whereas if I win I keep him? But Alex was already my son to start off with, so that makes me no better off. You'll have to think of something better than that, mate!"

"OK, how's this" said the king. "If I win the contest, I keep Alexander as my slave, but if you win, I will name him a Goblin Friend. I've taken a shine to him, I really have. That means I'll allocate some of my minions to be his guardian goblins, who will always be there to help him out, in case he ever gets into any magicky kind of trouble."

"A bit like a guardian angel? you mean " said Andrew."

The king hissed. "We don't use that kind of bad language. But basically yes."

"That sounds like a deal then" said Andrew, little realizing how many interesting complications this might cause later on. At this time, as you can imagine, his sole interest was to get Alex safe and home and tucked up in bed.

The king stepped forward and held out his right hand. It looked a bit revolting, but Andrew recognized the gesture, which was the same with human beings.

"Let's shake on it then" suggested the king.

Suddenly alarm bells went off in Andrew's brain, and he remembered something which he had read so long ago, it seemed like in another world.

"Not so fast mate" he said. "I remember doing GoblinPrudence in my first year studying law at Hull University. Let me think, what did it say?" He gazed up at the moon as if seeking inspiration, and his tone changed as he switched over to his posh lawyering voice.

"Domesday book, Northern edition, page 427, paragraph 2, the bit next to the ink stains at the bottom of the page....

Verbum Rex goblinorum bolluxus est. Sed vera quando libro scriptus writtus mustus.

Which, loosely translates as:- the word of a Goblin King isn't worth a fart:- unless it's written down."

"Bugger" said the king.

"My pen" said Andrew, and reached into the cavernous pocket of his great coat, from which he withdrew his special lawyering pen, made from the quill feather of a surprised goose. He also pulled out a bottle of permanent ink, some parchment, and a little folding riding table.

"You never know when these things will come in handy" said Andrew, by way of explanation to the gobsmacked onlookers. He quickly scratched together the appropriate legal phrases, signed his parts, and offered his quill to the king.

"If you would be so kind, your majesty, your autograph here, here and here."

Gunnar realized that he couldn't back down now, so he signed with a flourish. Then the witnesses queued up and signed. Then Andrew reached into another cavernous pocket in his great coat and pulled out a little battery operated Canon photocopier. After running off 3 copies to be retained by each party, each copy itself being marked with an "X" by 2 witnesses from each side, they were ready to proceed onto the deadly matter of the trial by combat.

the preduel contract

"Your choice of weapons, as the injured party is traditional" said the king. Drawing aside his coat to reveal a short goblin dagger at his belt.

Andrew already knew what he was going to choose.

"Blades" I think, said Andrew, and pulled out his old cavalry sabre from its leather scabbard.

"Agreed" said the king, with a sly grin as he unsheathed his little dagger.

It was only about six inches long, and Andrew was a bit surprised.

Andrew was a bit more than surprised a few moments later - when Gunnar flicked a switch on the handle of his dagger, and suddenly, as if by magic, out popped a six foot long horribly sharp, notchy sword with dark stains along the edge, like those really evil looking ones which the baddies always have in horror films.

"Oh shit" said Andrew, realizing he had been tricked.

They circled each other warily for a few seconds while the minions and the members of the hunt stepped a long way back our of harm's way. As innocent bystanders, they had no desire to get nicked or pricked or sticked by slashing blades in the moonlight.

"Let's begin then" said the king, as he poked forward with an exploratory lunge.

Andrew easily avoided that one. But he knew he had to be very careful. More than his own life depended on the outcome of this fight. If he lost, Alex would spend the rest of his days in the dark tunnels underneath the old Petersfield bookshop, only popping out, if he was lucky, to have a quick trip into the Waitrose car park, on the nights of the goblin meetings. (It wouldn't have been as bad as all that, but Andrew wasn't to know that the slave of a goblin king could have quite an interesting time.)

In the moonlight, their shimmering blades smacked together. They tinged and tonged and clattered and battered.

With his long sword, the king had a great advantage and he also had a lot more practice at sword fights (which he always won). The nearest that Andrew had ever come to waving a sword in anger, was when he was chopping wood with his axe for the fire. He realized that the king was winning, and if he didn't try something different soon he would be utterly defeated. He didn't fancy going home to tell Joanna that he had fought the goblin king and lost.

But Andrew was good at war games and tactics, and suddenly he got an idea. As they clashed an bashed, Andrew realized that timing was everything. Just as it looked like he was losing, and the king got ready for his final stroke Andrew called out...

"Your flies are undone!"

Too late, the king realized, even as he started to look down, that this was only a trick. That was the last thing that went through his mind as —— SWISH —— Andrew's sabre whizzed across from shoulder to shoulder.

The king's head popped twenty feet up into the air, and rolled away down the grassy slope landing in a rabbit hole. Then his body keeled over, stone dead. Not a twitch. And everyone fell silent.

A famous writer in Oxford who wrote about goblins, said that the game of golf was invented when the great Bullroarer Took, whacked off another goblin king's head in a place called the Shire. All I can say is, that Shire goblins and Wessex goblins are probably quite different, as we shall shortly see.

As I said before, everyone was stunned into silence.

Andrew wiped his sabre on his coat. There were lots of other revolting stains on the coat, so another one wouldn't really show. One of the goblin minions remembered to untie Alex, and just as he was handing him back to his father, a squeaky voice seemed to come from the rabbit hole.

"Someone get me out of here!"

It was the king, except his voice was higher. But they instantly obeyed.

"Someone put my head back on my body. No not that way around, you fools. That's better."

His voice dropped down to its normal deep pitch.

"Ah yes" he said by way of explanation. You've won, and all that, but luckily for me I guessed that your sabre was a traditional human one made out of steel."

He realized that Andrew didn't understand what he was talking about. He went on to explain.

"You see, if it had been made of silver, then instead of just having a bit of a sore throat for the next couple of weeks, I really would be dead."

He came up to Andrew to shake his hand.

"You won this fight, fair and square, by goblin standards anyway. I suppose I'll have to give up my idea of having a human slave. It's getting a bit unfashionable anyway. I think I'll have to get a BMW or a trophy wife instead."

"I can help you with that" said Andrew, hastily explaining "getting a good deal on a BMW, I mean."

"And you, my young man" the goblin king clasped Alexander's shoulder. "Alexander Woyte. I name you Goblin Friend. If anyone messes about with you or gives you gyp, just let me know, and I'll sort them out. I'll send some of my minions round later. They won't get in your way, but if you need them, just holler."

Nothing exciting happened on the way back to Privett.

Alex rode in the front of Andrew's saddle. Along the way, Andrew fell off. Alex stayed on. Andrew go back on. When they got home,

Alexander's mother already knew what had happened because someone in the hunt had phoned on their mobile.

The next evening, before Alex went to bed, his parents read him bedtime stories as usual.

The last one was "Good Night Gorilla."

It went through the litany of the "Good nights" finally ending with:-

"Goodnight Gorilla" read Mummy.

"Good night Alex" said Daddy.

"Good night Goblins" said Alex looking at the window.

There was a pause, then.

"Good night Alex" said the goblins.

They would always be there in the dark, making sure that he would come to no harm.

"Good night Alex" said the goblins.

the end...

That was the end of this story when it first happened. But it didn't stay the end forever. A year later there was a very much longer adventure for Alexander and his new goblin friends. Quietly now - because you don't want to undo the sleeping spell. But if you are curious and minded to creep ahead and explore... past the reviews and ads and the author bio you can see a short sample of the next story - which is called - Alexander White and the Pirates (and Goblins).

Now you may thinking - White? not Woyte? what's gone wrong here? And how come there's a typo right at the very beginning? In the second word of the title?

Despite what we've heard about the low editing standards of Indie ebook authors - and their tendency to retrain spilling chuckers to spell words the peculiar way they just typed them - surely this writer can remember how to spell the name of his leading character?

The explanation is this. By the time we got to the second adventure our hero was attending a slightly different and more grown up school.

2

reviews and letters from readers

in response to the goblinsearch edition 2001

Dear Mr. K.

Re your request for a favorable review from the Goblin Literary Review, the quote, below, is the best I could come up with. Hope you like it.

"In his story, Mr. K. uses a lot of words, which if rearranged in a completely different order, might make for **an interesting reading experience**."

Regards

Laszlo Screech (Editor)

PS - please make your cheque out payable to me personally, and not to the magazine. Thanks.

Dear Mr. Zsolt

Ref: HA/27312118/47G/ZK

Re Goblins mining tunnels under the shops in Petersfield.

Following our recent correspondence I am now satisfied that the aforementioned Mr Gunnar is in breach of the local planning regulations:- viz "change of use" from retail shop, to industrial mining, and that this was done without seeking planning consent. However, as you say that most of the tunnels were actually constructed sometime during the middle dark ages, i.e. before formal planning controls were in effect in this part of Hampshire, I am inclined to agree that a punitive levy of council tax may not be appropriate in this case.

We have therefore decided to rate Mr Gunnar's tunnels as "residential / goblin use", and as he has no windows, we have rated the property as band "F".

Can you please give me your assistance with another pressing matter. Unfortunately all the council tax demands sent to the address shown on the map in your story, addressed to Mr G have come back to this office marked as "Return to sender. Or else!" His telephone number also appears to be ex directory. Could you please give me his email address so that I can communicate to him the necessity of paying some form of local taxation.

Yours faithfully

Mr. Stoppem (Hampshire County Council Planning Dept.)

Dear Zsolt

Could you please mention somewhere on your web site, that my firm has now set up an dedicated team of lawyers and legal execs who deal in all aspects of the legal services relating to the special needs of pirates and goblins in the Portsmouth/Southsea area.

Yours sincerely
Andrew

PS - tell them not to contact us by email, which isn't set up yet. We prefer a letter or phone call, followed up by a working lunch.

PPS - Do you have Gunnar's new phone number? The pre nuptial contract for his trophy wife has been drawn up, but the copies of the documents I've sent him by post all get sent back unopened.

Dear Publisher

Re your request for an advertiser endorsement & other matters...

I am pleased to say that since we started advertising our patented hammers on goblinsearch.com, our sales in the USA have nearly doubled, despite the deepening recession over there.

It has also been useful to find out which side won the civil war, and we will change the wording when we reprint our brochures to remove the hint at uncertainty.

The advertising on your web site has been very cost effective, but I cannot recommend it to any of our competitors, because I don't want them to find out how well we're doing.

My fiancee, Darla, pointed out that the photo of me which you have on your web site, is not very flattering. I have therefore attached in this email, a much more handsome version which has been airbrushed to make me look better. Please replace the old one ASAP. Or else!

Yours
G. (Rex Goblinorum)

PS - Re your question about the overdue payment, I made some inquiries at this end and I assume that the cheque for the advertising got lost in the post.

It appears that one penny is not regarded as adequate postage nowadays, which came as a great shock to our post room. However, I have left instructions for my accounting minion to deal with it urgently when he gets back from his cruise in the Bahamas.

3

advert

Gunnar's Goblin Hammer
squishes troublesome pests fast

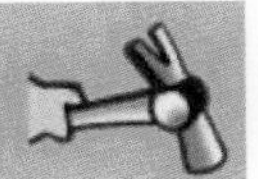

Are pesky goblin minions giving you gyp?

Ruining your picnics and Bar-B-Q's?

Squish 'em flat with Gunnar's patented Goblin Hammer.

Hello! - Gentle Reader

My name is Gunnar, King of the Old Wessex Division of the goblins. You've probably heard of me - because I was in that story Alexander Woyte and the Goblins.

And you're probably reading this ad, because you're being plagued by troublesome little goblin brats.

Relax! I've developed just the solution you need:-

Gunnar's Goblin Hammer!

I'm an expert at managing goblins, large and small. But the biggest problem comes from goblins when they're young (aged one to five) and haven't yet learned how to behave properly. In my job as King, I have to control hundreds of goblin minions, and they do exactly what I say - **or else!**

People often ask me about my management techniques and the best way to deal with troublesome goblin minion pests.

You know the sort of thing... It's a nice warm summer's day, and you're out in the garden, or up Box Hill enjoying a nice quiet picnic. Then you notice a sneaky goblin minion, scout hanging around, and before you know it, they're swarming all over the place, stealing your food and drinks.

Shouting at them doesn't work, because they think they're going to get away with it. Setting your dogs on them won't work, because little goblins taste disgusting. Kicking them doesn't help, either, because they're hard and will hurt your feet.

So I say:- **Squish 'em!**

Before I invented Gunnar's Goblin Hammer, the only methods which worked to control these little varmints were traditional and cruel. Skria's Goblin Skewer, and Loki's Electric Lighting Bolts were very effective at stopping a goblin swarm. They were good deterrents, but few of the actual victims survived, or if they did, they developed a life-long phobia about eating with forks or using electrical appliances.

Scientifically Proven:- My Goblin Hammer is based on years of painstaking research carried out mainly on stray visiting goblins from other counties in my secret underground goblin research laboratories at Hursley Park, near Winchester. My scientists discovered that a pressure of 10 tons per square inch is exactly the right amount to squish a young goblin flat.

Any less, and they spring straight back and just get angry.

Any more, and you risk being sprayed with goblin juice, and the victim may not survive to learn its lesson.

How to Order:- for security reasons, we don't ask you to give out your credit card details on the GoblinNet. All you have to do print out a copy of this ad, and leave it outside your back door in an empty milk bottle (or wine bottle) overnight with the correct money in cash (see below).

Delivery:- In the UK, and USA (except Alaska) we usually deliver it by 6 am next morning, and it's specially insured for 24 hours by a Spellabyte protective spell, so no-one else will be able to steal it. Your bottle will be returned with a receipt and guarantee.

Price:- UK - 25 Guineas. USA - 50 Dollars (Confederate , or Federal, *I forgot to ask which side won*). Europe, Asia and other regions:- we're currently looking for distributors. If you put a note out in a bottle, asking for the price, you should get a reply within a few days. (All payments in gold or silver please - we don't take paper currency, or plastic). Note:- if you live in a multi-tenanted building and can't safely leave bottles and money outside the back door, then another option is to leave it in the back seat of your car - clearly visible. My goblin minions are good at sniffing out orders, and will find it. You don't need to leave the car unlocked. They'll get in, without causing any damage, and leave the hammer on the back seat or in the boot.

Warning! Beware of cheap imitations! We never sell the Goblin Hammer in shops, fairs or by mail order. Using an incorrectly designed hammer doesn't work, and may be messy.

Anyone can use a Gunnar's Goblin Hammer. You don't need to be big or strong

features and benefits

- **works fast**:- so you can get back to enjoying your picnic
- **no special training required**:- full instructions, with pictures, supplied with every hammer (pack also includes 3 inflatable calibrated goblin minions to practise on)
- **acts as a deterrent**:- the mere sight of Gunnar's Goblin Hammer lying by your picnic or Barbecue is enough to make the little varmints go elsewhere
- **easier to use than traditional products**:- does not require sharpening, or electricity
- **environmentally friendly**:- no chemicals, or unpleasant odors, ozone friendly, dolphin friendly (can also be used to squish hammerhead sharks)
- **approved by the Goblins Cruelty League**:- squished minions reflate to their normal size and shape after about thirty minutes,suffering only from a mild head-ache
- **100 year no-quibble guarantee**:- (provided that hammer is returned by original owner, or heirs *in a clean condition please*)
- **warning - not to be used on adult goblins!** It doesn't work on goblins more than 6 years old. They'll just get annoyed, and may well try and use it back on you.

4

what's next?

Alexander White and the Pirates (and Goblins) - is a novel which takes place a year after the goblins first tried to kidnap the 4 year old Alexander. Now they're all friends - so what could go wrong?

First published in 2001 in another format – it will be available as an ebook in 2023

here's how it begins

It was February in Privett and it was raining.

In January it rained and washed away the first sprinkle of snow.

In December it had rained on New Year's Eve and made the bonfire go smoky. Alexander's godmother Janet had used her magic skills to light the fireworks, and the rockets still went up in the air with a bang, which surprised the brown chickens which had gotten into the habit of sleeping in the nearby yew hedge.

Alexander had to stand inside the garden shed out of the rain while the rockets were being aimed, and then dash out to see the trail of light flashing upwards into the sky. Then back in again to keep dry. The chickens in the hedge wondered if it would be all right for them to go inside as well. But they stayed in their nest, because they were suspicious of all this dashing about in the dark, and had heard rumors about a barbecue.

In November, before that, it rained and all the roads got flooded. Then some of the roads got renamed into rivers. Then some of the rivers got renamed into lakes. The swans were happy. But Alexander was not.

It seemed like it had been raining for ages. The last time it didn't rain was nearly a year ago, on the night when Alexander got kidnapped by the goblin king, Gunnar who lived in Petersfield. Alexander and the goblin king were friends now, ever since his father Andrew had come to the rescue and chopped the king's head off. That only kills a goblin king if the sword is made of silver, but that's another story.

A few days ago Alex asked one of his minders to ask the king if the goblins had anything to do with all the rain. The answer came back this afternoon in a letter delivered by registered goblin. Alex was too young to read it, so the messenger read it out for him. It said.

To: Alexander Woyte (Amicus Goblinorum)

Dear Alex

Regarding all this rain, and your question about whether the goblins have got anything to do with it....

The answer is.. No!

Yours sincerely

Gunnar, *Rex Goblinorum*

PS - I saw a program on *Red Hot Goblin* the other day. They said , it was "global warming". Hope that clears things up.

PPS - I hope my minions are looking after you. If they cause any gyp, let me know and I'll feed them to the dogs.

"What does that mean?" said Alexander.

Sleepsalot, one of the minions assigned to look after him, explained. - "The king doesn't like dogs."

The thought of global warming and the cold wet rain which rattled at the cottage's bedroom window made Alexander feel chilly. So, a few minutes after he was tucked up by his mother in the top bunk of his bed, when he was sure she had gone, he slid out again to put on a warm shooting jacket, his green warm hat, a pair of gloves and some fur lined boots. Then he climbed back up into his bed and snuggled in tight, being careful not to step on any goblins on the way up. Because his goblin minders were allowed to sleep on the lower bunk.

That's not how it started. But if you've ever got a new cat or dog in your house you know how this goes.

At first, his parents had made the goblins sleep outside the window, but with all the rain they used to get soaking wet, and their sneezing used to wake up everyone in the house, so his mother Joanna said they could sleep on the lower bunk of Alexander's bed, provided that they wiped their feet when they came in, and didn't have any "noisy" parties.

They kept to that part of the bargain, but sometimes such as on Alex's birthday or Christmas, they did have some "quiet" midnight parties which none of the grown ups knew about.

"Goodnight goblins" he said.

"Goodnight Alex!" chirped Eatsalot, the fat little goblin, who was still awake.

"Goodnight Alex..." yawned Sleepsalot, the thin little goblin who was trying hard to stay awake on guard duty.

"Bonsoir Alex" said Buvealot, a visiting Gallic Goblin who had done a student exchange with Lancelot the goblin who was visiting his long lost relations in San Marlo.

Lancelot's family had come over to Hampshire in the middle dark ages as a squire for the famous human knight known as

Lancelot du Lac, when he joined the court of King Arthur in Camelot (which as all goblins know was actually in Petersfield, and not in Winchester as most human historians mistakenly think).

Lancelot's singing was not as good in real life as it had been portrayed in the 1967 musical portrayed by Franco Nero. That was the real reason for the bust up between Arthur and his favorite knight. His singing was worse than a goblin karaoke night, and got on everyone's wick.

After a couple of bottles of Vin du Dark Ages Ordinaire, he would spend hours howling like a mad dog. The only way to shut him up was either to give him more to drink and hope he would pass out, or hit him over the head with another bottle (which was a lot quicker).

Squire Lancelot's heirs in England lost contact with their goblin cousins in (what later became) France - due to lots of human wars between the two countries - and a rare genetic tendency towards seasickness, which meant they avoided voyages if they had any choice in the matter.

Fifteen hundred years later - when the Channel Tunnel opened - connecting England to France without the use of wobbly boats - contact was reestablished between the separated goblin families and the modern Lancelot of Petersfield was welcomed as a long lost nephew by his Gallic cousins. Which was lucky for him as he avoided getting his feet wet.

That night - back on the top bunk of his bed - and wrapped up warm in his outdoor clothes - Alexander dreamt of water... and somehow his dream got mixed up with a strange site which was unfurling somewhere far, far away to the north...

How far north? Well my map doesn't go that far.

It was certainly much further north from Privett than Basingstoke, further north than the county (which would rather be a country) of Yorkshire, and even further north than Scotland, but not quite so far as the North Pole. Somewhere in that cold icy sea, where the Titanic met her doom nearly a hundred years earlier, global warming was having a drip, drip dripping effect on a funny looking iceberg.

Drip, drip splash, drip. It looked like a ship had once been caught in the ice and was now seeing the dawn sky for the first time in hundreds of years, as icicles hung from the rigging and then came crashing down like spears sticking in the wooden deck.

Crash. Shatter. Another one speared the deck, and then shattered.

Captain Feary had been watching these deadly ice shards crashing all around him through his one good eye (the left one without the patch, for the past ten minutes). He was wondering if he might be standing right beneath one of these ice skewers.

Crash, shatter. That one landed close. The trouble is, he was still frozen stiff and couldn't dodge out of the way. Crash, shatter. A small spike of ice stuck in the brim of his tricornered hat.

He couldn't remember how long he had been standing here watching the icicles melting. The last thing he remembered was being chased by those navy ships which had spotted them in the Irish Sea, and hung on their coat tails all the way up into the ice pack.

The navy boats gave up there. It was one thing to stake your chances on the outcome of a cannonade with a pirate ship. *That was glorious fun.* But only a foolish navy captain would risk his ship and reputation being mashed by a giant ice cube. So they hung around the edge of the ice field for a little while shooting off a few broadsides and starting avalanches all over the place just to show they had been there. And then they set sail back to sunny Portsmouth.

Captain Feary and his pirate crew had just broken out the rum to have a little celebration, when an ice storm hit them very suddenly. The alcohol in their blood had actually helped to preserve them and stopped their blood vessels from rupturing as they defrosted.

"Brrrr."

Behind him, Captain Feary heard someone shivering. So he was not the only survivor.

"Brrrr."

He couldn't turn round just yet, but he thought he knew who it was.

"Brrrr."

A warm breeze washed over the jolly pirate ship. Suddenly there was the tinkle of a thousand small splinters, and crack, crack, crack as the last sheets of ice broke off the sails, and suddenly Captain Feary found he could turn around and move.

"Brrrr" said the voice.

The Captain shook his crewman by the shoulder to speed up his circulation.

"Spit it out man. Don't hold it in."

Crack. His uniform defrosted. His lip was quivering.

"Shiver-mi-timbers" said Shiver-mi-timbers. "It's jolly cold here Captain."

Crash! Boing! A big lump of ice fell over the side of the ship, hit the gang plank (which was always fully extended) and bounced in the air before splashing down into the sea and waking up their giant towing shark, which, too, had been frozen underneath the boat all this time. With a great lurch, the shark tugged ahead and the ship broke away from the surrounding iceberg into the open sea.

In Alexander's dream the pirate ship looked vaguely familiar. In fact it looked very much like a big plastic pirate ship which he used to play with when he was three or four.

Come to think of it there was something strange about that shark. It looked a bit like the Action Man plastic shark which he had got for Christmas a few months ago. Except it was about a million times bigger.

This was turning into quite an interesting dream, so he turned over in the top bunk, and waited to see what would happen next...

About the Author

Zsolt Kerekes (spelling doesn't help you say it)

In February 2000 when I wrote the story Alexander Woyte and the Goblins I lived in Baughurst in Hampshire and worked on the internet as the editor and publisher of two computer publications:- the SPARC Product Directory and StorageSearch.com You can see what they were about by clicking the links which takes you to archived captures in the Internet Archive.

Since 2007 I've lived in East Chiltington in East Sussex where (in 2023) I'm writing an entirely new hard science fiction novel, rewriting an old goblin dystopia novella, and converting a bunch of my other stories from older formats into epub - or something close to it. This Alexander Woyte book was my first ebook conversion. Hopefully - as with past projects - it will get less bumpy as I learn how to use the tools in future releases.

Thanks for your time. Hope to see you again. If you've enjoyed this book please tell your friends about it. Book sales will enable me to spend more time writing.

Also by Zsolt Kerekes

these will appear as ebooks or audiobooks in 2023 / 2024

Alexander Woyte and the Goblins - 1st in the Alexander set

Alexander White and the Pirates (and Goblins) - 2nd in the Alexander set

Princess Laura and the Unsuitable Dragon Suitors

Jamie and the Tree Troll

My Pact with the Goblin Queen

The Goblins Are Coming!

Printed in Great Britain
by Amazon